The
RELUCTANT
DRAGON

The Reluctant Dragon

by Kenneth Grahame

Abridged and illustrated
by Inga Moore

WALKER BOOKS

AND SUBSIDIARIES

LONDON • BOSTON • SYDNEY

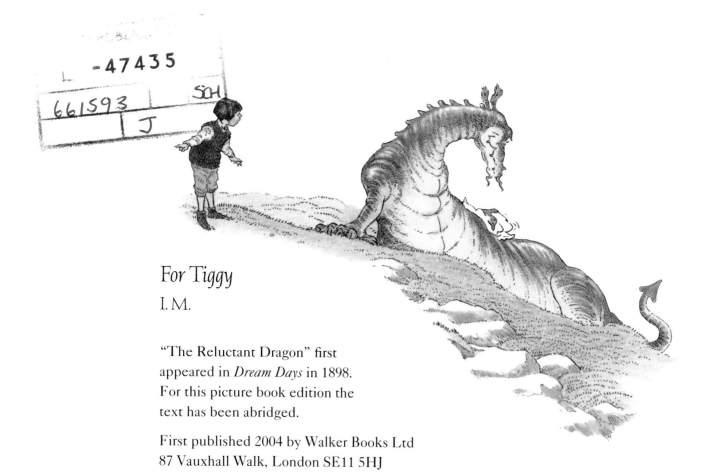

For Tiggy
I. M.

"The Reluctant Dragon" first
appeared in *Dream Days* in 1898.
For this picture book edition the
text has been abridged.

First published 2004 by Walker Books Ltd
87 Vauxhall Walk, London SE11 5HJ

10 9 8 7 6 5 4 3 2 1

Abridgement © 2004 Inga Moore
Illustrations © 2004 Inga Moore

The right of Inga Moore to be identified as
illustrator of this work has been asserted by her
in accordance with the Copyright, Designs and Patents Act 1988

This book has been typeset in Caslon Five-Forty

Printed in China

British Library Cataloguing in Publication Data:
a catalogue record for this book is available from the British Library

ISBN 0-7445-8638-0

www.walkerbooks.co.uk

FOREWORD

The Dragon in this story is so wonderfully funny and friendly (not to mention magnificent!) that anyone strolling on the Downs on a summer's day would count themselves very lucky indeed to find him lolling on the turf in front of his cave. I myself climbed up to the Downs near Uffington, in Oxfordshire, hoping to catch a glimpse. I was one of many visitors to that spot, famous for the ancient white horse which is etched into the chalk hillside and for the fight which, legend has it, took place there between the dragon and St George. I imagined Kenneth Grahame, who used to live near by, coming to this thrilling place and being inspired to write his delightful tale. Of course he wrote it a long time ago, but this heart-warming story of friendship between a dragon and a boy is as meaningful today as it has ever been.

Inga Moore

LONG AGO – oh, hundreds of years ago, it was – in a cottage by the Downs, a shepherd lived with his wife and their little son. Now, the shepherd spent his days – and sometimes his nights too – up on the wide, rolling, windswept Downs, with only the sun and stars and his sheep for company. But the Boy, when he wasn't helping his father, and often when he was as well, spent much of his time buried in books that he borrowed from the local gentry. His parents were very fond of him, and proud of him too. They knew that book-learning came in useful at a pinch, so they let him read as much as he liked. Natural history and fairy tales were what he liked mostly. And he would read them in a mixed-together, sandwichy sort of way – which is really rather a sensible way of reading.

One evening the shepherd, who had seemed on edge lately, and not his usual cheerful self, came home all of a tremble, and, sitting down at the table where his wife was sewing, he said:

"It's all up with me, Maria! Never no more can I go up on them Downs!"

"Why, what's the matter?" said his wife. "What can have got you so shook up?"

"You know that cave up there," said the shepherd. "I never liked it, and the sheep never liked it neither, and when sheep don't like a thing there's generally a reason. Well, there's been noises coming from it lately – sighings and grunts and snoring. So this evening I crept up and had a look – and I saw him!"

"Saw *who*?" asked his wife nervously.

"Why, *him*!" said the shepherd.

"Sticking half out of the cave, he was, as big as four carthorses, and all covered in shiny blue scales. Oh, he was quiet enough, not carrying on or doing anything – I admit that. And yet, *scales*, you know, and claws, and a tail for certain, well – I ain't *used* to 'em, and that's a fact!"

The Boy, who had been reading the story of *The Giant with No Heart*, closed his book, yawned, and said:

"Don't worry, Father. It's only a dragon."

"Only a dragon?" cried his father. "What do you mean, *only* a dragon? And how do *you* know so much about it?"

"I just do," replied the Boy. "You know about sheep, and weather, and things; *I* know about dragons. I always said that that was a dragon-cave. I always said it ought to have a dragon. In fact, I would have been surprised if you'd told me it *hadn't* got a dragon. Now, please, just leave this all to me. I'll stroll up tomorrow evening and have a talk to him."

"He's right, Father," said the sensible mother. "As he says, dragons is *his* line – not ours. It's wonderful him knowing about book-beasts. And if by chance that dragon ain't respectable, our Boy'll soon find out."

So next day, after he'd had his tea, the Boy strolled up the chalky track that led to the top of the Downs; and there, sure enough, he found the Dragon lying in front of his cave. He seemed peaceful enough. Indeed, as the Boy drew nearer he could hear him purring.

"Hullo, Dragon," he said when he got up to him.

The Dragon began to rise politely. But when he saw it was a boy, he frowned and said crossly:

"Now don't you hit me, or bung stones, or squirt water, or anything. I won't have it, I tell you!"

"Not going to," said the Boy. "I've simply looked in to ask how you are. But if I'm in the way I can easily clear out. Shan't shove myself in where I'm not wanted!"

"No, no," said the Dragon hastily, "don't go off in a huff. Fact is, I'm as happy up here as the day's long; always busy, dear fellow, always busy, I assure you! And yet, you know, between ourselves, it *is* a little dull at times."

The Boy sat down, bit off a stalk of grass and chewed it.

"Staying long?" he asked.

"Can't really say yet," replied the Dragon. "It seems a nice enough place, and I like the people – what I've seen of 'em – but I've only been here a short time, and one must look about before settling down. Besides – you'd never guess it – but the fact is, I'm *such* a lazy beast!"

"You surprise me," said the Boy politely.

"Oh, it's the sad truth," the Dragon went on, settling down between his paws, delighted to have found a listener at last; "and I fancy that's really how I came to be still here. You see, the other fellows were always fighting each other and so forth, and chasing knights all over the place, whereas I like to prop my back against a bit of rock and just think."

"What *I* want to know," said the Boy, "is what it *is* you like thinking about."

The Dragon blushed and looked away. Presently he said:

"Did you ever – just for fun – try to make up poetry?"

"Course I have," said the Boy. "Heaps of it. And some of it's quite good, I feel sure, only there's no one here who cares about it. Mother's very kind, when I read it out to her, and so's Father. But somehow they don't seem to—"

"Exactly," said the Dragon. "They don't seem to. Now you've got culture, you have, I could tell at once, and I should just like to read you a little sonnet I've been working on. I'm awfully pleased to have met you. I hope the other neighbours will be as friendly. There was a nice old gentleman up here last night, but he didn't seem to want to intrude."

"That was my father," said the Boy. "I'll introduce you if you like. But, look here, when you talk of neighbours and settling down and so on, I can't help feeling that you haven't actually thought things through. You see, there's no getting over the fact that you're a dragon, and an enemy of the human race."

"Haven't got an enemy in the world!" said the Dragon cheerfully. "Too lazy to make 'em, for one thing."

"Oh, I do wish you would try to understand," said the Boy. "When the other people find you, they'll come after you with spears and swords and all sorts of things. The way they look at it, you're a scourge and a pest and a bloodthirsty monster!"

"Not a word of truth in it," said the Dragon, wagging his head solemnly. "Why, I wouldn't hurt a fly. Not unless," he added with a wink, "you count boring 'em to death with my poetry! Speaking of which – about this sonnet…"

"Oh, if you *won't* be sensible," said the Boy, "I'm going off home. I can't stop for sonnets; my mother's sitting up. I'll look you up tomorrow, and *do* try and realize that you're a pest and a scourge, or you'll find yourself in an awful fix. Good night!"

The Boy found it easy enough setting his
parents' minds at rest about his new friend.
Indeed, they took his word without a murmur.
The shepherd was introduced, and while his wife
could not bring herself to actually meet the Dragon,
she made no objection to her son spending the evenings
with him quietly, so long as he was home by nine o'clock;
and many a pleasant night they had, sitting on the grass,
while the Dragon told stories of old, old times,
when dragons were quite plentiful
and the world was a livelier place
than it is now, and life was full of
thrills and jumps and surprises.

However, the most modest and retiring dragon in the world, if he's as big as four carthorses, is bound to be noticed, and, as the Boy had feared, it was soon the talk of the nearby village that a real live dragon sat brooding in the cave on the Downs. Though the villagers were frightened, they were rather proud as well to have a dragon of their own. Still, all were agreed that this sort of thing couldn't go on. The countryside must be freed from this dreadful beast. The fact that not even a hen-roost had been harmed since the Dragon's arrival wasn't allowed to come into it. He was a dragon and he couldn't deny it. He was a scourge and a pest and he must be got rid of. But in spite of much talk, no hero was found willing to take up sword and spear. Meanwhile the Dragon lolled on the turf, told antediluvian tales to the Boy, and polished up his verses.

One day the Boy, walking into the village, found the little street was lined with people chattering, shoving and ordering each other to stand back.

"What's up?" the Boy asked a friend.

"*He's* coming," his friend replied.

"*Who's* coming?"

"Why, St George, of course. He's coming to slay the Dragon! Oh my! Won't there be a jolly fight!"

The Boy wriggled his way through to the front of the crowd and waited. Presently there came the sound of cheering and the measured tramp of a great warhorse as St George paced slowly up the street. The Boy's heart beat quicker and he found himself cheering with the rest, such was the beauty and grace of the hero. His golden armour gleamed, his plumed helmet hung at his side, and his fair hair framed a face gentle beyond telling, till you caught the sternness in his eyes. He drew rein in front of the inn, assuring the villagers that all would be well, that he would free them from their foe. Then he dismounted and went in through the doorway, and the crowd went pouring in after him.

But the Boy ran up the hill as fast as he could go.

"He's here, Dragon!" he shouted. "You'll have to pull yourself together and *do* something!"

The Dragon was busy polishing his scales with a bit of old flannel.

"Don't be *violent*, Boy," he said without looking round. "Sit down and get your breath, and then perhaps you'll be good enough to tell me *who's* coming."

"That's right, take it coolly. It's only St George, that's all," said the Boy. "I thought I'd warn you because he's sure to be round early, and he's got the longest, wickedest-looking spear that you ever did see!"

"Well, tell him to go away," said the Dragon. "I'm sure he's not nice. Say he can write if he likes. But I won't see him."

"But you've got to," said the Boy. "You've got to fight him, you know, because he's St George and you're the Dragon."

"My dear Boy," said the Dragon. "I've never fought anyone in my life and I'm not going to begin now."

"But he'll cut your head off if you don't," gasped the Boy.

"Oh, I think not," said the Dragon. "You'll be able to arrange something. You're good at that. Just run down and make it all right, there's a dear chap."

The Boy made his way back to the village feeling very down-hearted, for if his dear friend the Dragon wouldn't fight, then St George would surely cut his head off.

"Arrange things indeed!" he muttered gloomily. "Why, the Dragon treats the whole thing as if it were an invitation to tea."

As he passed up the little street the villagers were straggling homeward in high spirits, eagerly discussing the splendid fight that was in store.

St George now sat alone in the inn, musing on his chances in the fight, and the sad tales of robbery and wrongdoing that had been poured into his sympathetic ear.

"May I come in, St George?" said the Boy politely, pausing at the door. "I want to talk to you about the Dragon."

"Yes, come in, Boy," said the Saint kindly. "Another tale of misery and wrong, I fear me. Is it a kind parent, then, of whom the Dragon has bereft you? Or some tender sister or brother?"

"Oh, no – nothing of the sort," said the Boy. "The fact is, this is a *good* dragon."

"Aha – a good *dragon*," said St George, smiling pleasantly. "I quite understand. Believe me, I don't mind in the least that he is no feeble specimen of his loathsome tribe."

"But he *isn't* loathsome," cried the Boy. "He's a *good* dragon, and a friend of mine, and he tells me the most beautiful stories you ever heard, all about old times and when he was little. And he's been so kind to Mother; and Mother'd do anything for him. Father likes him too. The fact is, nobody can help liking him, once they *know* him."

"Sit down, and draw your chair up," said St George. "I like a fellow who sticks up for his friends, and I'm sure the Dragon has his good points. However, history teaches us that the most charming of fellows can be the greatest rascals, and all evening I've been listening to tales of murder, theft and wrong."

"Oh, those villagers," said the Boy, "they will tell you anything. All they want is a fight. They're the most awful beggars for getting up fights – dogs, bulls, dragons – you name it, so long as it's a fight. And I've no doubt they've been telling you what a hero you are, and how you're bound to win and so on; but let me tell you, I came down the street just now, and they were betting six to four on the Dragon!"

"Six to four on the Dragon," said St George sadly, resting his cheek on his hand. "This is an evil world, and I begin to think that not all the wickedness in it is bottled up inside the dragons. But what are we to do? Here we are, the Dragon and I, almost face to face, each supposed to be thirsting for the other's blood. I don't see any way out of it."

"I suppose," said the Boy, "you couldn't just go away quietly, could you?"

"Impossible, I fear," said the Saint. "Quite against the rules. *You* know that."

"Well, then," said the Boy. "It's early yet – would you mind strolling up with me and seeing the Dragon, and talking it over? It's not far."

"Well, it's irregular," said St George, "but it seems about the most sensible thing to do."

"I've brought a friend to see you, Dragon," said the Boy.

The Dragon, who had been snoozing in front of his cave as they arrived, woke up with a start.

"This is St George," said the Boy.

"*So* glad to meet you, St George," said the Dragon. "You've been a great traveller, I hear. I've always been rather a stay-at-home. But if you're stopping, I can show you many interesting features of our countryside—"

"I think," said St George, in his frank, pleasant way, "that we ought to get down to business and sort out this little affair of ours. Don't you think that, really, the simplest plan would be to fight it out and let the best man win? They're betting on you, down in the village, you know, but I don't mind."

"But there's nothing to fight about," said the Dragon. "And anyhow I'm not going to, so that settles it!"

"Supposing I make you?" said St George, rather nettled.

"You can't," said the Dragon. "I should only go into my cave and retire for a time. You'd soon get sick of waiting outside. And the moment you'd gone, why, out I'd come again, merrily, for I tell you, I like this place and I mean to stay!"

St George gazed at the fair landscape. "But this would be a beautiful place for a fight," he began again. "These great bare rolling Downs for the arena – and me with my golden armour showing up against your shiny blue scales! Just think what a picture it would make!"

"You can't get at me that way," said the Dragon. "It won't work. Not that it wouldn't make a pretty picture as you say," he added, wavering a little.

"You see, Dragon," said the Boy, "there's got to be a fight of some sort. You can't want to go and stop in that dirty old cave till goodness knows when."

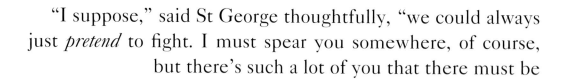

"I suppose," said St George thoughtfully, "we could always just *pretend* to fight. I must spear you somewhere, of course, but there's such a lot of you that there must be a few *spare* places where it wouldn't hurt. Here, for instance, behind your foreleg. It wouldn't hurt here."

"No, no," said the Dragon coyly. "It would tickle – it would make me laugh and that would spoil everything."

"Let's try somewhere else, then," said St George. "Under your neck, for instance – all these folds of thick skin. If I speared you here you'd never even know I'd done it!"

"Yes, but are you sure you can hit the right place?" asked the Dragon anxiously.

"Of course I am," said St George. "You leave that to me."

"Look here, Dragon," interrupted the Boy, "what I want to know is, if there's to be a fight and you're licked, what do *you* get out of it?"

"Tell him, please, St George," said the Dragon. "What *will* happen after I'm vanquished in deadly combat?"

"Well, according to the rules I shall lead you in triumph down to the market-place."

"And then?" said the Dragon.

"And then there'll be speeches and things," continued St George. "And I shall explain that you're converted, and so on, and see the error of your ways."

"Yes, yes. Quite so," said the Dragon. "And then?"

"Oh, and then," said St George, "why, and then there'll be the usual banquet, I suppose."

"Exactly," said the Dragon, "and that's where *I* come in. I'm going into society, I am. Once people see the likeable sort of fellow I really am, why, I shall be invited everywhere. So now that's all settled, and if you don't mind – don't want to turn you out, but…"

"Remember, you'll have to do your proper share of the fighting, Dragon!" said St George, as he took the hint and turned to go. "I mean ramping, and breathing fire and so on!"

"It's surprising how one gets out of practice," said the Dragon, "but I'll do my best. Good night!"

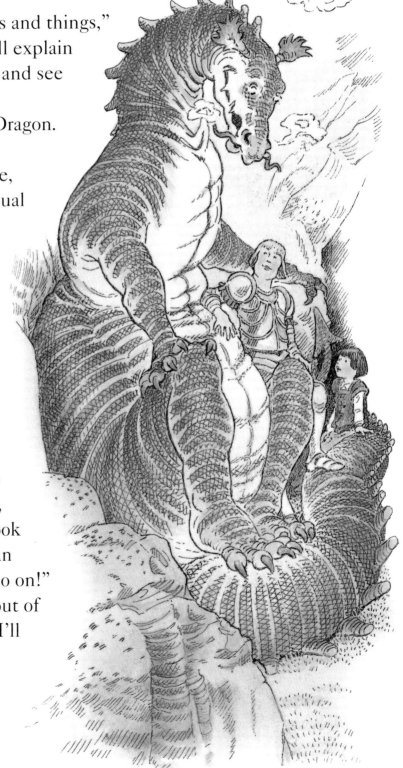

Next morning the people began streaming up to the Downs
at an early hour, in their Sunday clothes and carrying baskets
with bottle necks sticking out of them. Places were chosen
and the higher ground was soon thick with sightseers.

The Boy found himself a good place, well up
towards the cave. He was feeling anxious.
Could the Dragon be depended upon?
He might be too nervous to show up.
There was no sign of him in the
cave. Could he have done
a moonlight flit?

Presently the sound of cheering
told him something was happening.
A minute more and St George's red plumes
topped the hill. The Saint rode slowly forth
on his tall warhorse, his great spear held erect,
the little pennon, crimson-crossed, fluttering at its point.
He drew rein and waited.

The crowd leaned forward expectantly.

"Now then, Dragon!" hissed the Boy. And the Dragon, who,
it turned out, had liked the idea of play-acting immensely,
and who had been up since dawn rehearsing his part,
was not about to let him down.

A low rumble, mingled with snorts, was heard;
it rose to a bellowing roar that seemed to fill the air.
Clouds of smoke billowed from the mouth of the cave
and then the Dragon himself, shining, sea-blue, magnificent,
pranced splendidly forth; and everybody said, "Oo-oo-oo!"
His scales were glittering, his long spiky tail lashed his sides,
and his claws tore up the turf and sent it flying high over
his back, and smoke and fire jetted from his nostrils.

"Oh, well done, Dragon!" cried the Boy.

St George lowered his spear, bent his head, dug his heels
into his horse's sides and came thundering over the turf.
   The Dragon charged with a roar and a squeal –
a great blue whirling combination of scales
and snorts and clashing jaws and spikes.

"Missed!" yelled the crowd. There was a muddle
of golden armour and blue scales and a spiky tail,
and then the great horse, tearing at his bit,
carried the Saint, his spear swinging,
almost to the mouth of the cave.

The Dragon sat down and barked viciously,
while St George with difficulty pulled his
horse round into position.

End of round one, thought the Boy.
How well they both pulled it off,
and what a good play-actor
the Dragon is!

At last St George managed to get his horse to stand steady, and, looking round as he wiped his brow, he caught sight of the Boy and smiled and nodded.

The Dragon, meanwhile, was using the interval to give a ramping performance in front of the crowd. Ramping, it should be explained, consists of running round and round in a wide circle, sending waves and ripples of movement along the whole length of your spine, from your ears right down to the spike at the end of your tail.

"Time!" yelled everybody.
The Dragon left off his ramping
and began to leap from one side
to the other with huge bounds.
This naturally upset the horse,
who swerved violently. The Saint
only just saved himself, and as they
shot past, the Dragon snapped viciously
at the horse's tail, which sent the poor
beast careering madly over the Downs,
so that the language of the Saint,
who had lost a stirrup,
could fortunately
not be heard.

In round two the crowd were clearly warming to the
Dragon. They liked a fellow who could hold his own so well;
and many encouraging remarks reached the ears of our friend
as he went strutting to and fro, his chest thrust out and his tail
in the air, hugely enjoying his new popularity.

St George had dismounted and was tightening his girths,
and telling his horse exactly what he thought of him.
So the Boy made his way down to the Saint's end
and held his spear for him.

"It's been a jolly fight, St George!" he said.
"Will it last much longer?"

"I think not," replied the Saint. "The fact is, your silly
friend's getting conceited, now they've begun cheering him.
He'll soon start playing the fool, and there's no telling where
it will stop. I'd better get it over with this round."

He swung into his saddle and took his spear
from the Boy. "Now don't you worry," he said.
"I've marked the spot exactly."

St George shortened his spear, bringing
the butt well up under his arm; and, instead
of galloping as before, he trotted smartly up
to the Dragon, who crouched, flicking his
tail till it cracked like a great cart-whip.

The Saint wheeled and circled round
his opponent, keeping his eye on
the spare place; while the Dragon
paced slowly and very warily beside
the Saint, feinting from time to time
with his head. So the two sparred
for an opening, while the crowd
held their breath.

Though the round lasted for some minutes, the end was so swift that all the Boy saw was a lightning movement of the Saint's arm, and then a whirl of spikes and claws and flying bits of turf. The dust cleared, the crowd whooped and ran in cheering, and the Boy saw that the Dragon was down, pinned to the earth by the spear.

It all seemed so real that the Boy ran in breathlessly, hoping the dear old Dragon wasn't really hurt. But as he drew near, the Dragon lifted one eyelid and winked solemnly. He was held fast to the earth by the neck, but the Saint had hit the spare place agreed upon, and it didn't even seem to tickle.

"Bain't you goin' to cut 'is 'ead orf, mister?"
asked one of the crowd. He had backed the Dragon,
and naturally felt a little sore.
"There's no hurry," replied St George.
"I think we'll go down to the village first,
and have some refreshment, and then
I'll give him a good talking to,
and you'll find he'll be
a very different Dragon!"

At that magic word *refreshment* the whole crowd formed up in a procession and waited for the signal to start. St George, hauling on his spear, released the Dragon, who rose and shook himself and ran his eye over his spikes and scales and things, to see that they were all in order. Then the Saint mounted and led everybody back to the village, with the Dragon following meekly in the company of the Boy, while the thirsty crowd kept respectfully behind.

After refreshment St George made a speech, in which he told the villagers that he had freed them from their direful foe, and at a great deal of trouble and inconvenience to himself. So now they weren't to go about grumbling and pretending they'd got grievances, because they hadn't. And they should not be so fond of fights, because next time they might have to do the fighting themselves, which wouldn't be the same thing at all. Then he told them that the Dragon had been thinking it over, and saw that there were two sides to every question, and he wasn't going to do it any more, and if they were good perhaps he'd stay and settle down. So they must make friends, and not be prejudiced and go about thinking that they knew everything, because they didn't, not by a long way. And he warned them about the sin of making up gossip and thinking other people would believe them. Then there was much repentant cheering. And then everyone went off to get ready for the banquet.

Banquets are always pleasant things, consisting mostly, as they do, of eating and drinking; but the specially nice thing about a banquet is that it comes when something's over, and there's nothing more to worry about, and tomorrow seems a long way off. St George was happy because there had been a fight and he hadn't had to kill anyone; he didn't really like killing, though he often had to do it. The Dragon was happy because there had been a fight, and far from being hurt in it he had won popularity and a sure footing in society. The Boy was happy because there had been a fight, and in spite of it all his two friends were on the best of terms.

And all the others were happy because there had been a fight, and – well, they didn't need any other reason. The Dragon took great pains to say the right thing to everybody, and proved to be the life and soul of the party; while the Saint and the Boy, looking on, felt as if they were merely guests at a feast held entirely in honour of the Dragon. But they didn't mind, being good fellows, and the Dragon was not in the least bit forgetful. On the contrary, every so often he leant over towards the Boy and said: "Look here! You will see me home afterwards, won't you?" And the Boy always nodded, though he had promised his mother not to be out late.

At last the banquet was over. The guests had dropped away with many good nights and invitations, and the Dragon, who had seen the last of them off, went out into the street followed by the Boy. He sighed, sat down and gazed at the stars.

"Jolly night it's been!" he said. "Jolly stars! Jolly little place this! Think I'll just sit here for a bit. Don't feel like climbing up that hill just yet."

St George, who was outside strolling in the cool night air, saw them sitting there – the great Dragon and the little Boy.

"Now look here, Dragon," said the Saint firmly. "This little fellow is waiting to see you home, and you *know* he ought to be in bed by now, and what his mother'll say I *don't* know."

"And so he *shall* go to bed!" cried the Dragon, getting up. "Poor little chap. Fancy him being up at this hour! Why, it's a shame, that's what it is! But come along, let's have no more of this shilly-shallying. Off we go – that's the way."

So they set off up the hill,
the Saint, the Dragon and the Boy.
The lights in the little village began to
go out; but there were stars, and a late moon,
as they climbed to the Downs together.

And, as they turned the last corner and
disappeared from view, snatches of an old song
were borne back on the night breeze. I can't be certain
which of them was singing, but I *think* it was the Dragon!